Big Country Fair

D0981676

Hillsboro Public Library
Hillsboro, OR
A member of Washington County
COOPERATIVE LIBRARY SERVICES

For Ava and Ruby.
Also for my sensational sisters,
Tash, Katie and Claire. xxx

First published in 2016
by Faber and Faber Limited
Bloomsbury House
74–77 Great Russell Street
London WC1B 3DA

Designed by Faber and Faber
Printed in Europe
All rights reserved
Text © Pip Jones, 2016
Illustrations © Ella Okstad, 2016
The right of Pip Jones and Ella Okstad to be identified as author
and illustrator of this work respectively has been asserted in
accordance with Section 77 of the
Copyright, Designs and Patents Act 1988

This book is sold subject to the condition that it shall not,
by way of trade or otherwise, be lent, resold, hired out or
otherwise circulated without the publisher's prior consent
in any form of binding or cover other than that in which
it is published and without a similar condition including this
condition being imposed on the subsequent purchaser
A CIP record for this book is available from the British Library

978–0–571–32070–7
2 4 6 8 10 9 7 5 3 1

33614080733123

MIX
Paper from
responsible sources
FSC® C022612
FSC
www.fsc.org

Squishy McFluff
The Invisible Cat

Big Country Fair

by *Pip Jones*

Illustrated by *Ella Okstad*

FABER & FABER

Can you see him? My kitten?

He's a sight to behold!

He's stunningly fluffy.

(And also quite bold!)

Imagine him, quick!

Have you imagined enough?

Oh good! You can see him!

It's Squishy McFluff!

It was a Sunday in autumn

and young Ava's room

Was filled with the scents

of her mummy's perfume.

The floor was all covered

with ribbons and bows

And there on the bed,

next to Ava's best clothes,

Squishy McFluff

was invisibly curled.

4

Ava squealed: 'You're the

cutest cat in the world!

'But we still need to blow dry

your fur, and my hair!

''Cos it's only two hours

'til the Big Country Fair!'

The hairdryer BLASTED

and over the hum,

Ava just about heard

a loud shout from her mum:

'Er, AVA? Do you REALLY

need my entire

'Manicure set? And can I

have my hairdryer?

'I need to get ready.

My hair is still wet!'

But Ava said: 'Sorry, Mum!

Not finished yet!

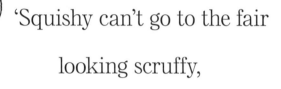

'Squishy can't go to the fair

looking scruffy,

'He has to be handsome

and **perfectly** fluffy.

'I'm using your nail files

to shape all his claws.

'He needs scent on his whiskers,

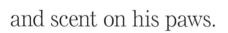

and scent on his paws.

'Today is the day

we'll achieve our ambition

'To come FIRST in the

Prettiest Pet Competition!'

Mum sighed, grabbed a towel,

and rubbed her damp head.

'I'm not sure you should enter him,

Ava . . .' Mum said.

'While I do understand

Squishy's special to you,

'The judge might

not "see" Squish

the same way

you do.'

Well, Ava was just far

too busy to listen.

She buffed Squishy's claws

'til they started to glisten.

She fluffed up

his tail

and she powdered

his nose.

'You're ready!' cried Ava.

'Now, practise your pose!'

Squishy pounced! And he

    landed upon Ava's desk,

Struck a glamorous stance

    (which was quite statuesque),

With his nose in the air,

    and his eyes shining bright . . .

'Perfect!' said Ava.

'You're a winner, alright!'

Downstairs, Daddy said:

    'So, you're finally ready?

'Good. Fill this bag up

    with all your old teddies.

'Choose the ones you don't want

    and we'll donate them all

'To the lady who's running

    the teddy bear stall.'

Taking the bag,

Ava tramped back upstairs,

Where she and McFluff

looked at all of her bears.

17

'Oh, crumpets!' said Ava

in a sad little voice.

'This is ever so hard.

No, I can't make a choice!

'Just look at them, Squishy.

Which ones should go?

'I think YOU'LL have to choose,

'cos I really don't know!'

Squish thought for a moment . . .

then (silently) miaowed.

'I agree,' Ava said.

'Oh yes, Dad WILL be proud!'

Then Ava and Squishy McFluff

filled the sack.

They bounded downstairs,

where they had a quick snack,

21

Before setting off

(full of anticipation)

With Mum, Dad and Roo,

to the local bus station.

They arrived at the fair

at a quarter to one.

The whole field was packed

with great ways to have fun.

A big hot dog stand!

Toffee apples to try!

There were donkeys to pet!

And a coconut shy!

A policeman was letting

the kids try his hat!

'Ooh, Squish!' Ava whispered.

'Just look at THAT!

'Candy floss! Yum!

Watch the man make it twizzle!'

. . . But the candy floss flopped

when it started to drizzle.

Mummy dashed under

an oak tree for shelter,

But Squishy had spotted

the big **helter skelter!**

'Please, Daddy!' whined Ava.

'Look! There's no queue!'

Dad groaned, but then came

a voice Ava knew:

'I'll take you! I just need to

check I have cash . . .'

'Hooray!' Ava shouted.

She squeeeezed Auntie Tash,

Then gasped as she set eyes on

Tash's wheelbarrow.

Inside was a HUGE . . . no,

a GINORMOUS marrow!

'The Giant Veg Contest,'

Tash said with a grin.

'It's my biggest one yet!

Do you think I might win?'

'Oh YES!' Ava said.

'And I hope Squish will too,

'In his Prettiest Pet

Competition debut!'

'He's BOUND to win, poppet!'

Auntie Tash cried.

'Now, let's go and have a

quick turn on that slide.'

Wheeeeee! Off they went!

They whizzed round and round!

They twisted and turned

as they sped to the ground,

Then landed – FAH-LUMP!

– with a bump and a thud.

'Oh NOOOO!' Ava shrieked.

'Squishy's covered in mud!'

'He won't win first prize

with fur muddy and flat!'

'Hmm,' Daddy said.

'Listen, never mind that.

'You have plenty of time to,

erm, get Squishy ready.

'Look, there's Mrs Ayres!

Let's donate your teddies.'

They walked through the fair,

as the big grey clouds parted.

'It's just great to donate,'

Dad said. 'Very kind hearted.'

Ava opened her bag,

and she placed on the stall

Just one little teddy.

It was so VERY small,

Mrs Ayres had to wear her thick

glasses to see.

She put on a price tag,

and wrote on it: 'Free'.

'That's ALL?' Mummy asked.

'You brought ONE? Is that right?!'

'It's Squishy!' said Ava.

'He NEEDS bears at night.

'And the bag Daddy gave me

was already stuffed

'With these pampering things

that I need for McFluff!'

'McFluff or McMischief?'

Mum sighed. Then she smiled.

'Right, I'll get some tea

while you get Squishy styled.'

'Oh, your FUR!' Ava frowned.

Squish pawed at her pocket . . .

'You're RIGHT Squish,' said Ava.

'Let's find a plug socket!'

They hadn't gone too far

before Squishy spied

Just what they needed.

'We'll soon have you dried,'

Ava said, as she plugged

   Mummy's hairdryer in.

The thing BLASTED and

   hummed and so, over the din,

She did not hear the shouts.

   She did not hear the gasping.

She did not hear the hiss

   or the very loud RASSSSPING!

Ava had not a CLUE

of the chaos created,

On the big bouncy castle . . .

which had promptly DEFLATED!

Ava jumped

  as the loud speaker boomed:

'ARE THE PRETTIEST PETS

  ALL PAMPERED AND GROOMED?

'THE PET COMPETITION

  IS READY TO START!'

'This is it, Squish!' said Ava.

  Thump! Thump! Thump! went her heart.

McFluff took his place.

Ava glanced down the line.

'Don't worry!' she told him.

'Squish, you'll be just fine!

'There are rabbits and dogs,

a rat and a budgie.

'And there's one other cat,

but it's snotty and pudgy!'

The mayor (who was judge), said:

    'A poodle! So curly!

'With a great pom-pom tail . . .'

    Ava said: 'It's quite GIRLY,

'My kitten's more stylish . . .'

The mayor, looking stern,

Just held up her hand and said:

'Please, wait your turn!'

'How exotic!'

the mayor said,

stroking a parrot.

'And this bunny!

So sweet how it

munches

its carrot . . .'

'My cat's teeth aren't GOOFY . . .'

Ava quietly mumbled.

'Ssshh! Wait your TURN!'

the grumpy mayor grumbled.

At LAST the mayor came,

and asked: 'Where is your pet?'

As she waved round the sparkly

first-prize rosette,

And stood

there, confused,

looking puffy

and stout.

'Well? WHERE is this cat

　　you've been bragging about?'

'Er, he's THERE,' Mum said, pointing.

　　'And Ava IS smitten . . .

'But McFluff's a rare breed

　　of INVISIBLE kitten.'

'Ooooh!' cooed the crowd. Then,

'Hmmm,' said the mayor.

'Well, in that case, I'm very

pleased to declare

'That first prize today

goes to Reggie the Rat.'

'WHAT?!' Ava shrieked,

as she scooped up her cat.

'His tail's like a . . . WORM!

That's not fur, it's just FRIZZ!

'Oh, why can't you all see

how CUTE Squishy is?

'Well, I KNOW he's the best.

We don't NEED that prize!'

She ran off with Squish . . .

and with tears in her eyes.

Sitting so sadly, just behind

the marquee,

Where people were drinking

their hot cups of tea,

Ava hugged Squishy,

and let out a snuffle.

But then she heard yelling.

It was quite a kerfuffle!

'My marrow! My marrow!

Oh, HELP! It's been taken!'

It was Auntie Tash shouting!

She sounded quite shaken.

'Oh nooo!' Ava said.

McFluff pointed his paw.

Ava looked, and there

in the distance she saw

A man making off with a

wobbling wheelbarrow,

Which contained Auntie Tash's

prize-winning marrow.

'STOP! THIEF!' yelled Ava,

running after the man.

'You've been caught red-handed.

We've foiled your plan!'

'You think YOU can stop me?'

the thief asked. 'You can't!'

'That marrow,' said Ava,

'belongs to MY AUNT.

'I might be quite little . . .'

(Ava's voice had gone shrill),

64

'But if I cannot stop you . . .

I BET MY CAT WILL!'

'So WHERE,' sneered the thief,

'is this fierce cat of yours?'

McFluff strrrretched . . .

then bared his invisible claws.

One steely eye twitched,

and so did a whisker,

While Ava (quite creepily)

started to whisper:

'Behind you, behind you!

Mind where you stand!

'He's right by your shoe!

Now he's sniffing your hand!

'He's jumped on your shoulder!

His tail's in your EAR!

'Look harder! Turn quicker!

No, not THERE . . . he's here!'

'WAAAAH!' the man screamed.

'Oh! I'm being attacked!'

He made such a racket,

he began to attract

The attention of people

all over the fair.

'The thief!' a man bellowed.

'Hey, you! Stop right there!'

'HELP! Get this cat off!

It's too quick to catch!'

The thief kept on shrieking,

while trying to snatch

At Squishy McFluff

(who could NEVER be caught).

Then Mummy ran over!

And with her she brought

Dad, Auntie Tash,

the policeman, the mayor.

Then a whole bunch of people

turned up to stare.

The policeman said: 'Sir!

Now, don't make a fuss.'

And, quick as a flash,

he had the thief in handcuffs.

'You saved my marrow, Ava!'

Auntie Tash cried.

'It was Squishy, not me,'

Ava proudly replied.

'Your invisible kitten,' said the mayor,

'stopped the thief?

'A rare breed indeed!' she exclaimed.

'Well, good grief,

'I declare a brand NEW prize,

never won yet,

'For the Country Fair's Bravest

INVISIBLE Pet!'

'Wow!' Ava said.

The mayor took, as she spoke,

An invisible medal

from the folds

of her cloak.

'And Ava – I hope you don't

have one already –

'But, to say thank you, here's a . . .

GIGANTIC TEDDY!'